SYRACUSE
UNIVERSITY®
BIG BOOK OF
BASKETBALL ACTIVITIES

Peg Connery-Boyd

 sourcebooks
jabberwocky

 Hawk's Nest
Publishing, LLC

Published by Sourcebooks Jabberwocky, an imprint of Sourcebooks, Inc.
P.O. Box 4410, Naperville, Illinois 60567-4410
(630) 961-3900
Fax: (630) 961-2168
www.sourcebooks.com

Source of production: Versa Press, East Peoria, Illinois, USA
Date of production: September 2016
Run number: 5007322

Printed and bound in the United States of America.
VP 10 9 8 7 6 5 4 3 2 1

LABEL THE PARTS OF A BASKETBALL COURT

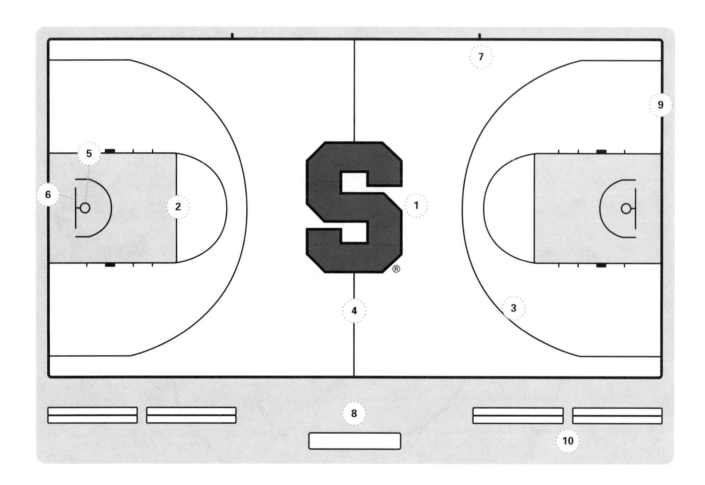

____ Center circle

____ Division line

____ Endline

____ Throw-in line

____ Three-point line

____ Backboard

____ Basketball hoop

____ Free throw line

____ Team bench area

____ Scorer's table

Solution is on page 52.

FOLLOW THE BALL
Which shot goes through the hoop?

Solution is on page 52.

CONNECT THE DOTS

SYRACUSE®

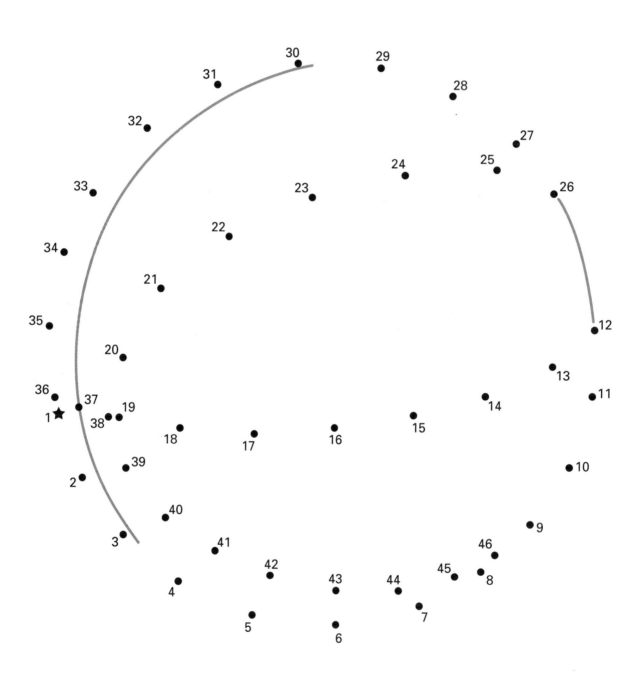

WORD SEARCH

```
H Z J B B C B N U R M T
M Y V O I F I C C F G H
T U A T O M G Z A D X N
O A M T I Z H H R G Q R
T R W O J E E W R I C O
N M A I R W A Y I W E L
S Y A N M G D H E H W J
I M K S G X S O R I K S
R Z F W C E O H M T D N
R O W Y N O A J A E X V
A L E Q X F T B K T G Q
O Y Q I C U S E H N J X
```

ARMY	'CUSE®	ORANGE®
BIG HEADS	DOME	OTTO
CARRIER	MASCOT	WHITE

Solution is on page 52.

LET'S SOLVE!

Help the player dunk the ball!

START HERE

Solution is on page 52.

FIND THE DIFFERENCES

Can you find all three differences between the two images below?

Solution is on page 53.

LET'S DRAW!

Use the grid to draw the *Orange*® logo!

WORD SEARCH

H	F	P	F	I	L	X	U	Q	V	H	Z
I	R	E	T	I	P	O	F	F	T	Z	E
L	V	O	D	G	T	T	M	G	L	L	A
R	P	Y	U	R	A	O	C	R	W	M	R
Q	A	R	N	L	I	M	J	E	P	V	Q
W	Y	E	K	A	Y	B	P	T	A	N	M
C	Q	B	L	Y	S	A	B	H	S	B	U
B	H	O	N	U	Y	H	K	L	S	L	B
H	J	U	M	P	S	H	O	T	E	Z	Z
E	O	N	Q	H	E	Q	I	O	I	V	F
L	K	D	R	I	V	E	F	W	T	V	T
O	D	W	X	C	N	M	Y	L	G	D	S

DUNK	SHOOT	LAYUP
DRIVE	PASS	JUMP SHOT
DRIBBLE	REBOUND	TIP-OFF

Solution is on page 53.

_ _ _ _ _ (E)

_ _ _ _ _

_ _ _ _ !

KEY

 = A   ORANGE = I   O (Otto) = O   S = T

 = E   SU = L   'CUSE = P   (basketball) = Y

SYRACUSE = H   (whistle) = N   (jersey) = R

SCRAMBLE

Unscramble the letters of these signals demonstrated by the referees below.

TTSAR CLKCO

_ _ _ _ _   _ _ _ _ _

NUBOS RFEE WORTH

_ _ _ _ _   _ _ _ _   _ _ _ _ _

LANINTTENIO LFUO

_ _ _ _ _ _ _ _ _ _ _   _ _ _ _

TYHTRI DSENCO TMITEOU

_ _ _ _ _ _   _ _ _ _ _ _   _ _ _ _ _ _ _

RHETE TNOPI METTPAT

_ _ _ _ _   _ _ _ _ _   _ _ _ _ _ _ _

EETRH ONIPT LUFSUCSSEC

_ _ _ _ _   _ _ _ _ _   _ _ _ _ _ _ _ _ _ _

Solution is on page 54.

SCRAMBLE

Unscramble the letters of these courtside snacks.

ROCPOPN

_ _ _ _ _ _ _

CIE MCEAR

_ _ _ _

_ _ _ _ _

DOAS

_ _ _ _

ZEPRTEL

_ _ _ _ _ _ _

IAZPZ

_ _ _ _ _

OTH GDO

_ _ _ _ _ _

Solution is on page 54.

CONNECT THE DOTS

SYRACUSE®

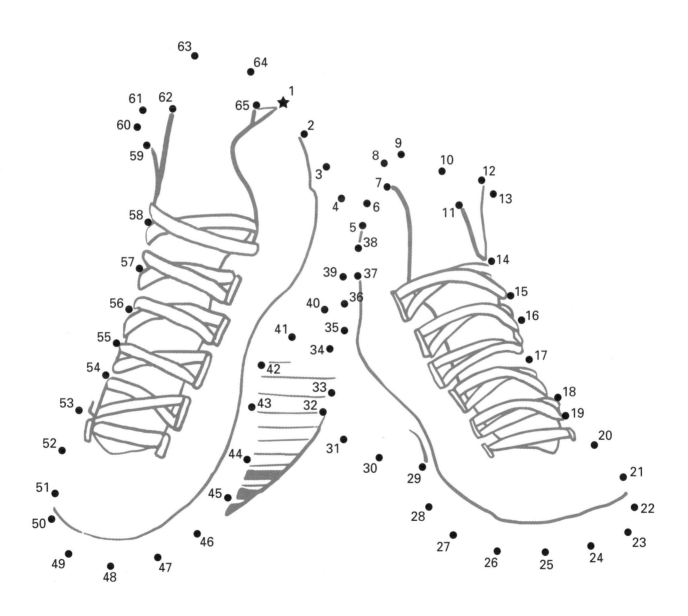

GOING FOR THE REBOUND!

WHAT'S THE SCORE?

Add the points to find out which team won the game.

SYRACUSE®

1ST HALF

HOME **44** 00:00 VISITOR **25**
B ◄ PERIOD 1 ▷ B

2ND HALF

HOME **20** 00:00 VISITOR **34**
B ◄ PERIOD 2 ▷ B

FINAL SCORE

HOME 00:00 VISITOR
B ◄ PERIOD 2 ▷ B

Solution is on page 54.

THE OPENING TIP-OFF!

WORD SEARCH

```
C H E E R L E A D E R S
T F U C F B K X E Y F P
S E A A O T X F F V G Q
S A A L R A H B E D V J
O Y H M W O C E N T E R
Q H S D A F I H S D E P
M L Q G R F Y Y E Y S P
G V Q X D E N G G S Z A
U E Z I X N V D T A T W
A F S U B S T I T U T E
R I N C P E A R X V U T
D L B W M K Y E L D D E
```

CENTER	DEFENSE	OFFENSE
CHEERLEADERS	FORWARD	SUBSTITUTE
COACH	GUARD	TEAM

Solution is on page 55.

CROSSWORD PUZZLE

Use your knowledge of the *Orange*® to solve the puzzle.

Across

2. The *Syracuse*® *Orange*® play in the Atlantic Coast _____.

3. The student section at *Syracuse*® games is called *Otto's* _____™.

6. In 2003, *Syracuse*® defeated the *University of* _____ to win the NCAA National Championship.

7. The home of the *Orange*® basketball team is the _____ *Dome*®.

8. _____ is a *Syracuse*® tradition that earns fans free tacos when the team scores 70 points.

Down

1. Which state is home to *Syracuse University*®?

4. The official colors of *SU*® are _____ and white.

5. *Otto the Orange*® is the *Syracuse*® _____.

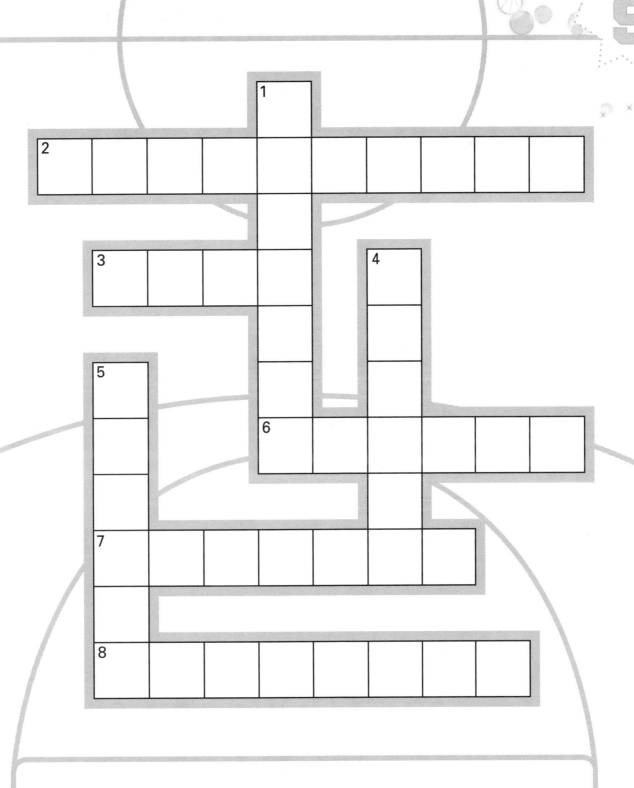

SECRET MESSAGE
Use the key to decode the message.

N _ _ _ _ _ _
  ORANGE 'CUSE

_ _ _   _ _ _ !
  ORANGE   ORANGE

KEY

= B	= H	= O
= E	'CUSE = I	ORANGE = T
= G	= N	= U

20   **Solution is on page 55.**

I HAD A GREAT DAY AT
CARRIER DOME.

by _____

It was a _____ day in _____.
(weather word)   (month)

The *Orange*® were playing the _____ at
                                (team name)

Carrier Dome®. We took a _____ to get to
                          (car / train / bus)

Syracuse. I snacked on some _____ and
                              (food)

_____ while we watched the game. I was
(food)

so excited to see _____ play
                        (player name)

today. He's my favorite player! The *Orange*®

_____ the game. The score was ____ to ____.
(won / lost)   (score)   (score)

Basketball is my favorite sport, but I also like to

watch _____. I can't wait to come back to
      (sport)

Carrier Dome®!

POPCORN

LET'S DOODLE!

Design your own pair of basketball shoes.

HINT!
Trick out your kicks with a cool pattern—use your imagination!

SCRAMBLE

Unscramble the letters of these basketball words.

PHOO

_ _ _ _

LWEHTIS

_ _ _ _ _ _ _

LLBASBATEK

_ _ _ _ _ _ _ _ _ _

EERFERE

_ _ _ _ _ _ _

YEJSER

_ _ _ _ _ _

RWEAT BLETTO

_ _ _ _ _

_ _ _ _ _ _

YPLARE

_ _ _ _ _ _

KSNEARSE

_ _ _ _ _ _ _ _

Solution is on page 56.

WHAT'S IN A NAME?

How many words can you make using letters found in the three words below?

THE CARRIER DOME®

Example: TRACER   ICE

1. _____   11. _____

2. _____   12. _____

3. _____   13. _____

4. _____   14. _____

5. _____   15. _____

6. _____   16. _____

7. _____   17. _____

8. _____   18. _____

9. _____   19. _____

10. _____   20. _____

WORD SEARCH

```
P T D S M O Q W Z W U B A
G E A L L E Y O O P O U F
E C D Y U J F N U A D Z G
E H K O F H F H J E S Z X
M N Q I W U A J Z W W E T
N I N T I N S L N R I R L
U C Z N H I T E F L S W G
M A T D I O B O I T H Y P
A L L D A Y R X W S I S B
B F Y U N A E O I N H M Q
E O V M X R A R F N V H E
Z U B L O C K V C O I L T
I L U T I G Y A C A U H I
```

ALL DAY	BUZZER	HALFTIME
ALLEY-OOP	DOWNTOWN	SWISH
BLOCK	FAST BREAK	TECHNICAL FOUL

Solution is on page 57.

WHAT'S THE SCORE?

Add the points to find out which team won the game.

SYRACUSE®

1ST HALF

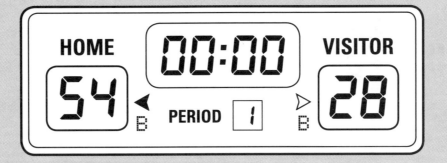

HOME **54** | 00:00 | VISITOR **28** | PERIOD 1

2ND HALF

HOME **26** | 00:00 | VISITOR **30** | PERIOD 2

FINAL SCORE

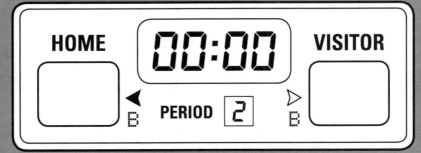

HOME | 00:00 | VISITOR | PERIOD 2

Solution is on page 57.

SECRET MESSAGE

Use the key to decode the message.

__ __ __ __ __ __ E ʼ

SYRACUSE.   ORANGE.   'CUSE.

__ __ __ __ __ ʼ

  SU. SU.

__ __ __ __ __ !

  SU. S.

KEY

= B	= E	'CUSE. = L	= S
= C	= H	SU. = O	= T
SYRACUSE. = D	ORANGE. = I	S. = R	

28   **Solution is on page 57.**

HIDDEN PICTURE

Use the key to color the shapes below and reveal the hidden picture.

KEY

G = Gray   **Bk** = Black   **O** = Orange   **W** = White   **Bl** = Blue

HINT!
Color inside the lines!

MY BASKETBALL CARD

SIDE 1:
Draw yourself!

(your name)

#
(number)

SYRACUSE®

SIDE 2:
Complete your stats!

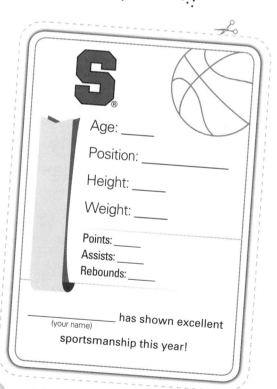

Age: ____

Position: ____

Height: ____

Weight: ____

Points: ____
Assists: ____
Rebounds: ____

_____ has shown excellent
(your name)

sportsmanship this year!

CROSSWORD PUZZLE

Use your knowledge of college basketball
to solve the puzzle.

Across

2. A player scores when he shoots the ball through the
   _____.

5. A college basketball _____ measures 94 feet
   long by 50 feet wide.

6. Each successful foul shot is worth _____ point.

8. What color are most basketballs?

Down

1. The referee blows a _____ to stop the action.

3. The game goes into _____ if the score is tied
   at the end of the game.

4. When you play on your own basketball court,
   you are the _____ team.

7. A jump _____ begins every college
   and NBA game.

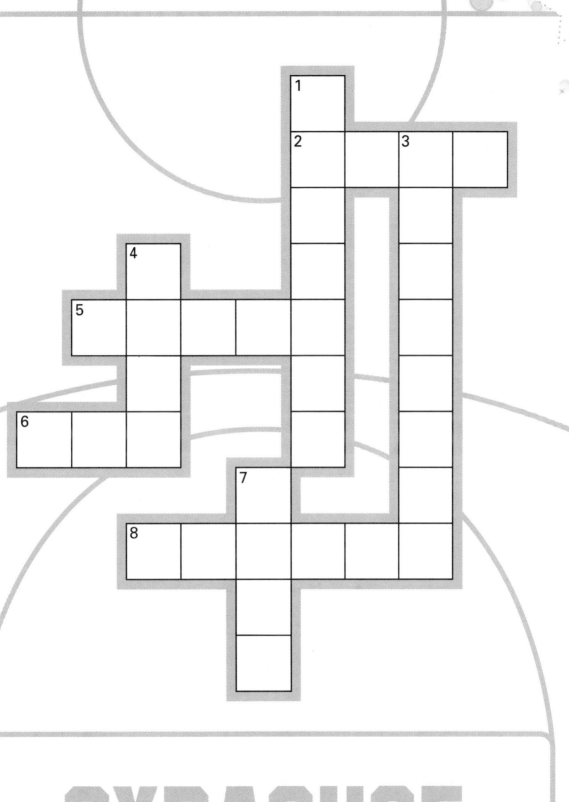

Solution is on page 58.

___ ___ ___ ___

___ ___ ___ ___   ___ ___ ___ ___

___ ___ ___ ___ !

KEY

🟠 = A	'CUSE = H	S = T
🏀 = B	ORANGE = K	🪈 = W
SU = E	👟 = L	🛹 = Y

Solution is on page 58.

LET'S MATCH!

Match the name of the play to the correct player.

DUNKING

DRIBBLING

SHOOTING

BLOCKING

PASSING

Solution is on page 59.

LET'S SOLVE!

Help the player make the shot!

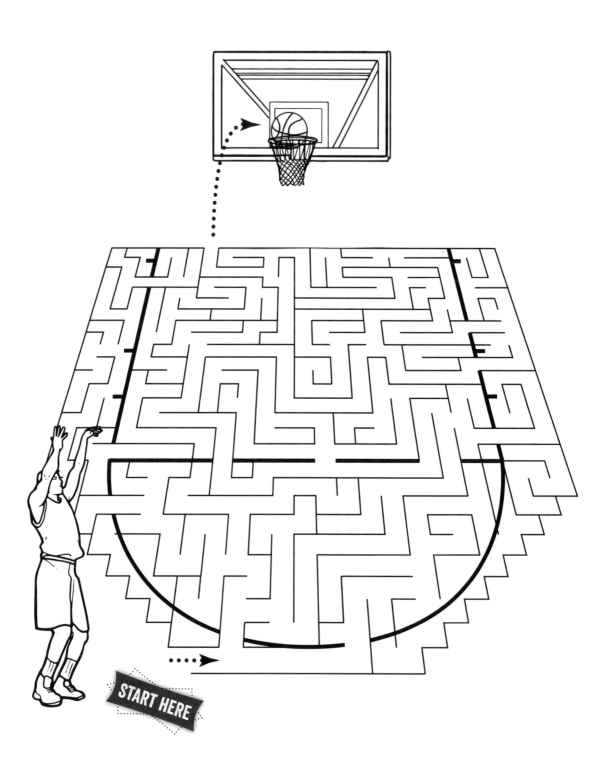

START HERE

Solution is on page 59.

FIND THE DIFFERENCES

Can you find all three differences between the two images below?

Solution is on page 59.

WORD SEARCH

```
C O U M A D N E S S Q V
M R Z E W T G M E D B F
U A W S T U L K B Z G X
G N R I Y F I B Q N O T
A G I C Z R L L G J O A
D E H V H E A O E J R C
F N Z G E S W C A F A O
L A F Z I R G K U Q N T
S T R O V E S J R S G I
I I V V U S G I M W E M
Z O H M Q A U G T F L E
D N A B G V X R X Y S Y
```

BLOCK
GO ORANGE®
MADNESS

MARCH
ORANGENATION™
SU®

SYRACUSE®
TACO TIME
UNIVERSITY

Solution is on page 60.

WHAT'S THE SCORE?

Add the points to find out which team won the game.

SYRACUSE®

1ST HALF

HOME **50** — 00:00 — VISITOR **30**

B PERIOD *1* B

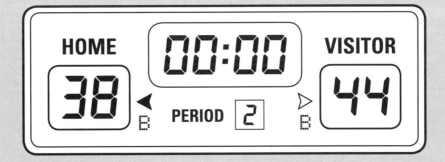

2ND HALF

HOME **38** — 00:00 — VISITOR **44**

B PERIOD *2* B

FINAL SCORE

HOME — 00:00 — VISITOR

B PERIOD *2* B

Solution is on page 60.

LET'S SOLVE!

Help the player drive to the hoop!

START HERE

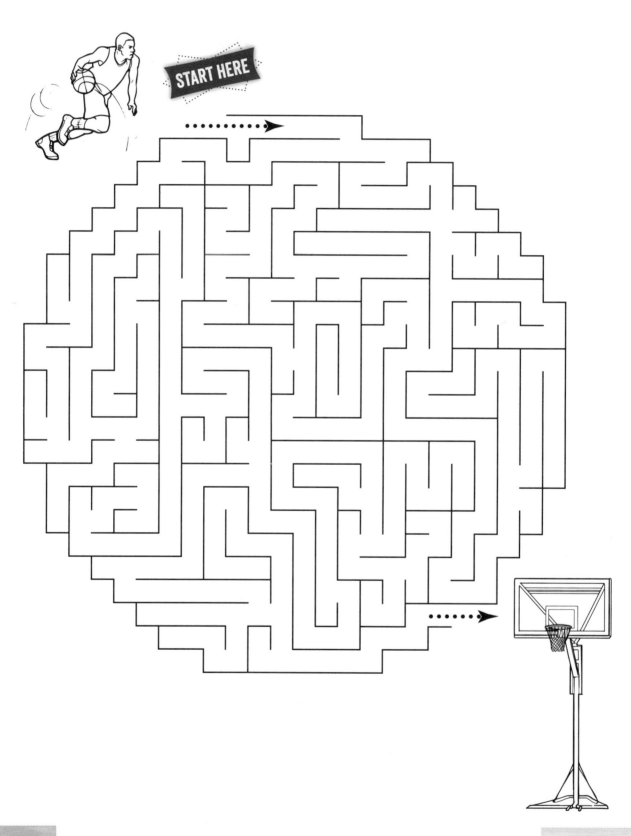

Solution is on page 60.

'CUSE®

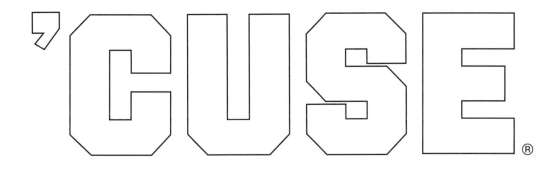

NEW YORK'S S COLLEGE TEAM™

FOLLOW THE BALL

Which ball does the player snag for the rebound?

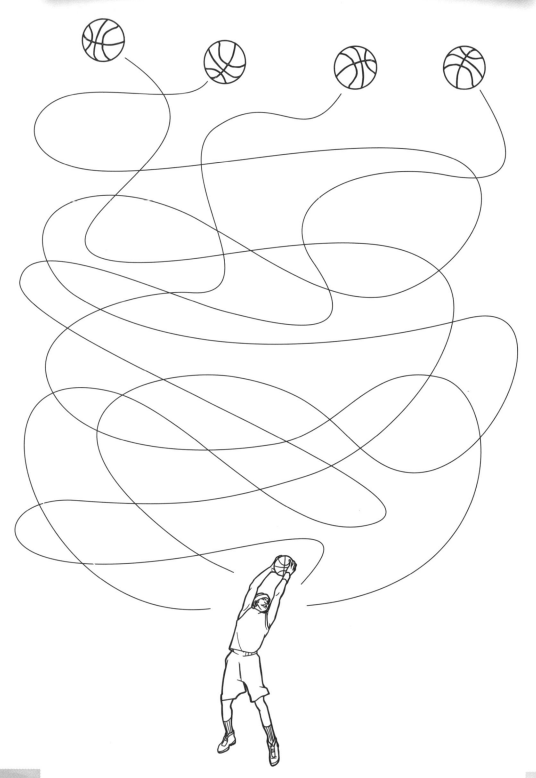

Solution is on page 61.

ORANGE® **S** SYRACUSE®   SU®

_ _ _ _ _ E

   SU®

_ _   _ _ _

_ _ _ _

KEY

ORANGE® = D	SYRACUSE® = I	**S** = R
SU® = E	= O	(whistle) = T
(shoe) = H	(backboard) = P	(basketball) = V

Solution is on page 61.

WORD SEARCH

```
B D U T M X W Q D U D S
E B O H C H P X Q L S G
G X E M G O T I D C C A
N W O N S O E P H U O R
O E U C C P T V C S R Q
D K T L W H I S T L E U
C T F O U L L I N E B O
X K Z C Z G E R X R O Z
C U X K E Y B R Y T A Z
Z Y N Q J D H R F I R K
S P B A C K B O A R D S
C C J N F C U T V B Y D
```

BACKBOARD	FOUL LINE	NET
BENCH	HOOP	SCOREBOARD
CLOCK	KEY	WHISTLE

Solution is on page 62.

CROSSWORD PUZZLE

Use your knowledge of college basketball to solve the puzzle.

Across

3. The _____ decides when to send in a substitute player.

5. A shot that goes in just before the signal for the end of the period is called a "_____ beater."

7. Players sit on the _____ when they are not playing in the game.

8. The _____ is usually the tallest player on the team.

9. A point _____ runs the team's offense on the court.

Down

1. Players leap for the _____ to retrieve the ball after a shot is missed.

2. The _____ keeps track of the points scored for each team.

4. The U.S. National _____ is played before every basketball game.

6. The _____ calls the fouls.

WHICH **SYRACUSE**® **ORANGE**®
IMAGE IS DIFFERENT FROM THE REST?

  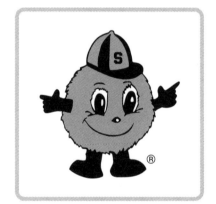

Solution is on page 62.

BASKETBALL BINGO!

Next time you're watching an *Orange*® game either in person or on TV, try playing this game! Simply cross off items as soon as you see them. If you cross off five squares in a row—vertical, horizontal, or diagonal—you win!

HALF-COURT SHOT	REFEREE BLOWING THE WHISTLE	DOUBLE DRIBBLE	THREE-POINT FIELD GOAL	FAN WITH A PAINTED FACE
FAN HOLDING A WHISTLE	LAYUP	PLAYER WEARING A SWEAT BAND	BLACK SNEAKERS	DOUBLE DOUBLE
FOUL	FAN EATING A HOT DOG	FREE SPACE	OVERTIME	PEP BAND
SWISH	MISSED FREE THROW	JUMP BALL	TEAM MASCOT	ASSIST
STEAL	WHITE SNEAKERS	SHOT CLOCK	REBOUND	BLOCKED SHOT

MY **ORANGE**® ROSTER

Fill in the blanks to complete your team's roster.

Season year _____

Head coach _____

_____
(name)

_____
(number)

Height: _____in

Weight: _____lbs

Position: _____

Hometown: _____

_____
(name)

_____
(number)

Height: _____in

Weight: _____lbs

Position: _____

Hometown: _____

_____
(name)

_____
(number)

Height: _____in

Weight: _____lbs

Position: _____

Hometown: _____

_____
(name)

_____
(number)

Height: _____in

Weight: _____lbs

Position: _____

Hometown: _____

_____
(name)

_____
(number)

Height: _____in

Weight: _____lbs

Position: _____

Hometown: _____

_____
(name)

_____
(number)

Height: _____in

Weight: _____lbs

Position: _____

Hometown: _____

_____
(name)

_____
(number)

Height: _____in
Weight: _____lbs
Position: _____
Hometown: _____

_____
(name)

_____
(number)

Height: _____in
Weight: _____lbs
Position: _____
Hometown: _____

_____
(name)

_____
(number)

Height: _____in
Weight: _____lbs
Position: _____
Hometown: _____

_____
(name)

_____
(number)

Height: _____in
Weight: _____lbs
Position: _____
Hometown: _____

_____
(name)

_____
(number)

Height: _____in
Weight: _____lbs
Position: _____
Hometown: _____

_____
(name)

_____
(number)

Height: _____in
Weight: _____lbs
Position: _____
Hometown: _____

_____
(name)

_____
(number)

Height: _____in
Weight: _____lbs
Position: _____
Hometown: _____

_____
(name)

_____
(number)

Height: _____in
Weight: _____lbs
Position: _____
Hometown: _____

BONUS!

★ **DRAW A STAR** next to the name of the team captain(s).

• **CIRCLE THE NUMBER** of the center.

■ **DRAW A SQUARE** around the name of the point guard.

SOLUTIONS

Page 2

1 Center circle
4 Division line
9 Endline
7 Throw-in line
3 Three-point line

6 Backboard
5 Basketball hoop
2 Free throw line
10 Team bench area
8 Scorer's table

Page 3

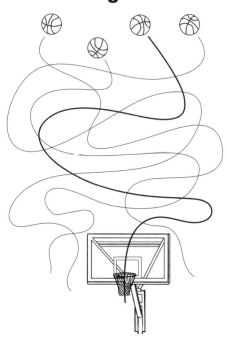

Page 5

```
H Z J B B C B N U R M T
M Y V O I F I C C F G H
T U A T O M G Z A D X N
O A M T I Z H R G Q R
T R W O J E E W R I C O
N M A I R W A Y I W E L
S Y A N M G D H E H W J
I M K S G X S O R I K S
R Z F W C E O H M T D N
R O W Y N O A J A E X V
A L E Q X F T B K T G Q
O Y Q I C U S E H N J X
```

Page 6

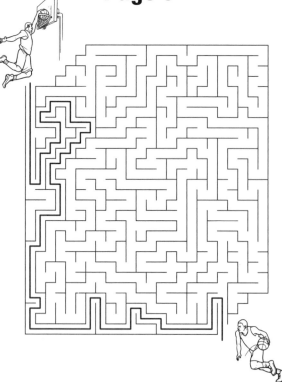

Page 7

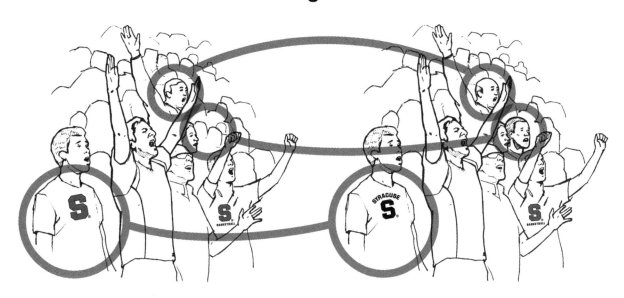

Page 9

Page 10

Page 11

START CLOCK

BONUS FREE THROW

INTENTIONAL FOUL

THIRTY SECOND TIMEOUT

THREE POINT ATTEMPT

THREE POINT SUCCESSFUL

Page 12

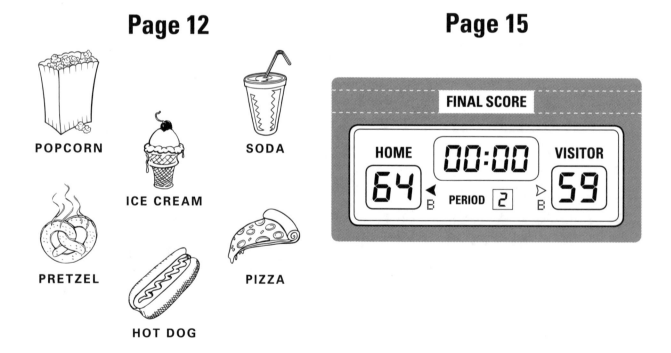

POPCORN

ICE CREAM

SODA

PRETZEL

HOT DOG

PIZZA

Page 15

FINAL SCORE

HOME
64

00:00

PERIOD 2

VISITOR
59

Page 17

Page 19

Page 20

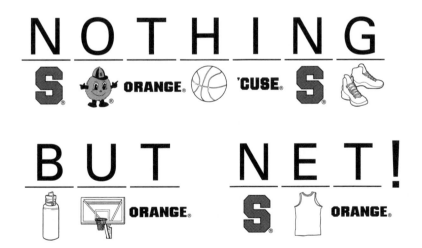

Page 24

HOOP

WHISTLE

BASKETBALL

REFEREE

WATER BOTTLE

JERSEY

PLAYER

SNEAKERS

Page 25

Below are just a few examples of words that could be made with these letters.

THE CARRIER DOME ®

ace	creed	hare	meet	rice
acre	dame	hat	mirror	ride
aim	dare	head	mode	roam
air	dart	hear	oat	tar
arc	dear	heart	ode	team
are	demo	hide	race	tear
car	doe	hire	raid	teem
card	dote	home	ram	tide
care	dream	iced	rare	tier
cart	ear	mare	read	tire
cream	era	mat	rear	trace
credit	hard	meat	red	tread

Page 26

Page 27

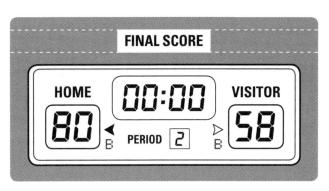

Page 28

DRIBBLE,

SHOOT,

SCORE!

Page 33

Page 34

TAKE

THAT   BALL

AWAY!

Page 35

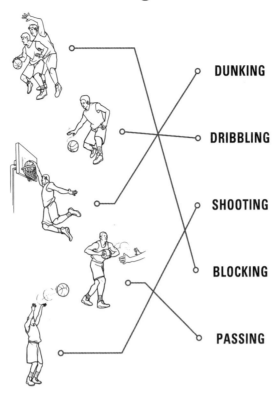

DUNKING

DRIBBLING

SHOOTING

BLOCKING

PASSING

Page 36

Page 37

Page 38

```
C O U  M A D N E S S  Q V
M R Z E W T G M E D B F
U A W S T U L K B Z G X
G N R I Y F I B Q N O T
A G I C Z R L L G J R A
D E H V H E A O E J A C
F N Z G E S W C A F N O
L A F Z I R G K U Q G T
S T R O V E S J R S G I
I I V V U S G I M W E M
Z O H M Q A U G T F L E
D N A B G V X R X Y S Y
```

Page 39

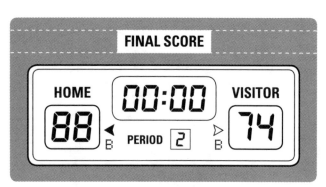

FINAL SCORE

HOME **88** ◄
B
00:00
PERIOD 2
VISITOR **74**
► B

Page 40

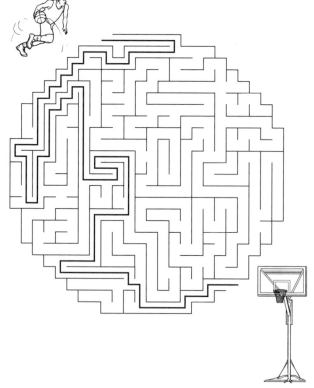

Page 42

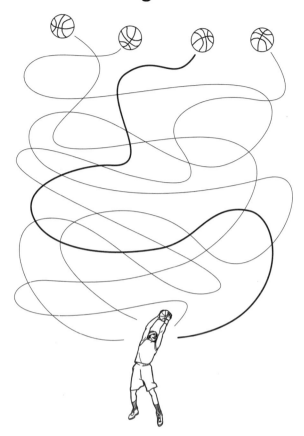

Page 43

D R I V E

ORANGE. **S** SYRACUSE. 🏀 **SU.**

T O   T H E

H O O P

Page 45

B D U T M X W Q D U D S
E B O H C H P X Q L S G
G X E M G O T I D C C A
N W O N S O E P H U O R
O E U C C P T V C S R Q
D K T L W H I S T L E U
C T F O U L L I N E B O
X K Z C Z G E R X R O Z
C U X K E Y B R Y T A Z
Z Y N Q J D H R F I R K
S P B A C K B O A R D S
C C J N F C U T V B Y D

Page 47

Across/Down crossword solution:

1. REBOUND
2. SCOREKEEPER
3. COACH
4. ANTHEM
5. BUZZER
6. REFEREE
7. BENCH
8. CENTER
9. GUARD

Page 48

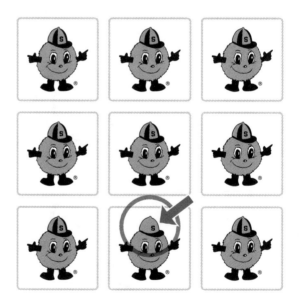